DRAC AND THE BLACK DRAGON

VINCE FOX

WESTBOW
PRESS®
A DIVISION OF THOMAS NELSON
& ZONDERVAN

WestBow Press books may be ordered through booksellers or by contacting:

WestBow Press
A Division of Thomas Nelson & Zondervan
1663 Liberty Drive
Bloomington, IN 47403
www.westbowpress.com
1 (866) 928-1240

ISBN: 978-1-9736-7092-6 (sc)
ISBN: 978-1-9736-7091-9 (e)

Print information available on the last page.

WestBow Press rev. date: 8/6/2019

Our Story begins with a young prince at the time when the land of Hungary and Romania were ruled by one king. Prince Drac Van Der Merwe was one of the most handsome and gifted men in all of Hungary. His skills as a warrior could not be matched by any other man or savage throughout the known land. Sadly, his pride and vanity of self could not be matched by the entire known universe. Drac's father Gottfrid Van De Merwe a great King with a contrite heart was caring and loving to his people as if they were his very own children. The King was also a great warrior that had kept the people safe from every kind of wicked creature that had ever tried to take over the kingdom. The King learned from his father and through his own hardships that after any victory on the battlefield that the flag of humility should be raised in their hearts so that no one would become prideful of the grace given to them that day.

King Gottfrids kingdom would grow ten times larger than that of his father's. His army was known throughout the land as "The Fire of the Dragon." This mighty force was spoken of throughout the world for their deeds were legend. The name of Gottfrid's army came from an event that had changed the King in many ways. You see dragons in his younger days were very fierce and hungry creatures that would feed on anyone and anything. The Kingdoms lived in fear for anyone could be snatched at any time by one of these flying creatures without a moment's notice.

Since these vicious creatures fed without warning, King Gottfrid had no other choice but to remove them from the land. At the same time these monsters were feeding on the people of Hungary their enemy's thought that this would be an opportune time to attack. Wicked men from distant lands traveled to destroy all that Hungary stood for and wipe them from the pages of history. A great battle took place on a fall day as the cries of suffering could be heard throughout the kingdom. King Gottfrids army was greatly outnumbered and hoards of the wicked were closing in on his already weary men. Hungary's battles with the great dragons had taken much of their strength for their campaigns had gone on for many years. King Gottfrid and his men had found themselves closed in on three sides with a large lake to their rear. The King knew if his men fled towards the water their armor would drown them and if they took off their protection the arrows of their enemies would easily bring them to their death. The King first ordered his men to close in shield to shield with their backs toward the water for at least no attacks would come from the rear. Then he once again looked around at the large numbers of the wicked that had traveled such a long distance to destroy him and his people. In great sorrow King Gottfrid began to cry out to the Lord for it had been over two years since he lost his father and the pain was still very present. Gottrid said "Father in heaven I'm so sorry if I've wronged you, show me the way and I will change. I know I'm not a perfect man, but I have always tried to honor your ways. If in doing my good deeds I've become prideful toward others I am sorry. Show me what pleases you and I will change". Then as tears began to run down his face, he stood and screamed up towards the heavens with great passion "I have not felt your presence in some time, if today be my last at least give me your presence!" Most of the world would never understand the cry of the king.

I f you have ever walked with the peace of the Lord then find it removed, you know you'll never be the same until you walk in that again. What the King didn't understand was that in his great despair God was drawing him closer even if he couldn't see or feel it. The little amount of self-effort that was left in the King would still get in the way of him giving the Glory to where it had always belonged.

The noise from this great battle had been shaking the ground for miles awaking man and beast throughout Hungary. The King tried his best to keep the morale of his men uplifted as they watched the sky begin to darken. Then with a great look of amazement the King said to himself "Why has the night come so early in the day" As the King continued to look towards the heavens he could now see far in the distance that the sky was filled with dragons of all kinds and they were flying in towards the battle. The Dragons were in great number as if the noise of the war brought every one of them out to feed from their dark caverns. The people of Hungary had been fighting off these creatures for some time and knew where their weak spots were located. But the enemies of Hungary did not because they had never battled beast like these. The King quickly thought to himself that these creatures may be exactly what he needed. He began to instruct all his men to run towards the lake and start removing their armor so that the weight would not drown them.

Hungary's enemies began to laugh with pride as they watched the Kings army enter the lake, this laughter quickly turned to horror as the dragons began to fly in snatching soldiers left and right. Fire could be seen throughout the landscape as the King and his men swam like never before. They received minor burns at times coming up from the water to take a breath, but fear had given them the ability to stay under for much longer that they normally could have. The encmies of Hungary were aiming for the head of the Dragons which is the hardest part of their body, so no damage was being inflicted. At one point the King noticed that the sky was not full of fire as it had been before, so he came up to see what had taken place. He was amazed to see all the casualties that where lying on the battlefield. He instructed his men to swim back towards their land. The King could see that his enemies figured out that thc area located under the dragon wing above the rib cage was its weak point due to the number of dragons that were found grounded. But this information was late in being discerned for not one of Hungary's rivals was left standing. As Gottfrid watched the last Dragons fly towards the sunset he ordered his men not to follow. The King stood there amazed thinking that things had looked so bleak earlier and how quickly they had changed. He then began to whisper "My Lord my heart was full of great despair, my hope was small. My faith may have been the size of the smallest seed. But here I stand amazed at what you have done by your own hand." The King would have never thought the thing that had terrorized them for so long would be the one thing that brought them their freedom. Then one of his soldiers yelled "Long live King Gottfrid of Hungary" At that time the rest of his army began to chant with passion those same words. But the King said to his men "By God's hand our enemies have brought us peace."

The King in his heart had no desire to remove another Dragon from the kingdom but knew if it meant protecting his people that he would do so. For whatever reason those remaining Dragons moved on from Hungary to unknown lands and were never seen again.

As time went on King Gottfrid and his army freed many villages and towns from evil men that forced their ways on to others. Gottfrid always preferred and fought to find peace with anyone he met on the battlefield, but some men hunger to rule the weak and power becomes something that they never get enough of. The bows of Hungary brought fire from the skies for those choosing war for Gottfrids archers were unmatched. The savages knew the legend of Hungary's army; when the sky was lit with fire it brought the wrath of the dragon. Many who fought against Gottfrid saw him as an evil conqueror due to their own warped view and pride.

The King played on this even further as he named his first son Drac which did not please his wife at first. He spoke gently to his queen as he held her hand and said "My dear this child would not have the breath in his lungs if it were not for those Dragons." which she then replied "I know that in our language Drac means dragon and I want to honor God with his Gift but Drac also means to many in our world Devil. Do you want others to see your son as a devil?" which then the King replied, "My dear, my precious queen sadly no matter what we call him our enemies will always see him as a devil". The queen understood that in the harsh world they lived in that she could only control the deeds of her own life. She knew that a name would not change the heart of any man so to honor the gift that saved her husband she agreed on the name of Drac.

Drac grew into a strong young man but with the long illness and death of his mother a slow turn to self-began to grow without him being conscious of it. Gottfrids army had become very powerful and his son Drac grew prideful due to their victories. The King's son could not see the favor of God on the battlefield but was blinded by believing in his own abilities to conquer any force that came against them. It didn't help the prince that his face and body looked as if they were made out of marble sculpted by the Greeks themselves. This would explain why most of the prominent women of the kingdom worshiped him and poured out words of flattery anytime they were in his presence. When the King was younger his father's army defeated forces much larger than they were. They could easily see where there praise for victory was to be given. But now that his force had become so great the King was worried that pride would grow in every victory. He also knew if his son did not put on humility that his men would also become blind and worship Drac for every battle won. The King was saddened to see that his son's heart was becoming dark due to all the victories that were given to him. He knew that the enemy of our souls, the evil one that was cast out of heaven wanted nothing more than to have our heart's preoccupied with the meaningless things of this world. The King feared Drac's love of self would be his destruction if he did not intervene.

G ottfrid knew that humility was the
greatest gift he could give his son that he
loved so dearly.

King Gottfrid called for his only child
and told him he was going to send him on
a quest. There was a village far away from
Hungary full of simple town's folk that needed training in the
art of combat. He told him "You are to go alone and train the
villagers so they can protect themselves from the horrors that
could come to them from unknown regions". Drac was furious
and would have no part to his father's plan. "I am to be King
father, are you so jealous of all my victories that you would send
me away! Am I not the greatest fighter that has walked the halls
of this castle?" Drac said. His father could see that it was far
worse than he had expected. "My son you threaten our servants,
disrespect every commoner you meet and disgrace the very
name Van Der Merwe. The generations before us had a heart
to serve their people but you have only a heart of self. Instead of
seeing how blessed we are you see it as entitlement something
you think you deserve. My dear son you have become blind to
those that choose to give their lives freely so that this kingdom
could serve those around us in need. Drac then said "Father,
why then has God blessed your son with such greatness" The
King replied "To serve the people my son but your gifts have
made you prideful and your heart has become blinded to your
sickness. Thankfulness, gratitude, Drac where are they to be

found, I see no signs of them in you and it breaks my heart. My son this Kingdom has never been about you or me it has always been about something much larger that either one of us. You will go now with one of our strongest steeds, fully equipped to travel to this distant land or be banished and leave this castle with only your name. Hopefully one day you will see that a father's love was at the heart of this discipline but my son you have left me with no other choice, now go." Screaming he stormed out of his father's throne room turning over the suit of armor that stood at the exit. He vowed never to return to Hungary and warned his father that he would be sorry for the decision he made today. As he was leaving the castle you could hear his rude remarks demanding the servants to get out of his way, one servant that had cooked his meals said quietly to himself "I guess you won't be eating breakfast in bed tomorrow your highness" as a great big smile grew across his face. The signs of relief were easily seen from both the servants and commoners when the news spread that Drac would be leaving the kingdom for a quest.

The older men working in the stables and the blacksmiths that once served the King in his army stopped their work to pay their respect to the prince as he was leaving. The prince could not understand why these men had such long faces as he stormed out by them all, they seemed so down hearted to Drac but then he thought nothing of it and continued in his rage. What Drac didn't know was that these men were also once great warriors some of the best that the kingdom had ever known with even greater odds against them than the prince had ever seen. They knew that this decision could not have come easily for the King to send his son that he loved so dearly away.

They also remembered their own prideful ways and the pain they endured in those early youthful years. One said with a mournful expression "It will be the most agonizing thing he's ever felt or gone through in his life, but he can be restored and healed if he humbles himself and does not harden his heart". They all stared down towards the ground for some time and thought about their own season of brokenness and the great suffering they endured, then went back to work.

Drac entered the Kings stable and saddled one of Hungary's strongest steeds and without the king's permission took another horse for supplies. The prince chuckled and said to himself "Yes father I'll leave but not without taking more than I need". As the young prince was heading out away from the castle his father could see him from his tower. The King looked up to the heavens and prayed "Father In heaven, I love my son with all of my heart, but he was yours before he was mine. You have a love that I still can't completely grasp, your ways are not my own. But you're a good father so I ask you to watch over my son and help me in my weakest moments of trust. Please help me to focus on your goodness so I don't give the evil one a place to put his thoughts".

The journey to this land would take months by horse and even longer with all the other dangers that could slow travel. Drac was already starting to feel the wear and tear of the long journey ahead of him but had no idea that things would soon get even worse.

On one occasion Drac's campsite was being destroyed by 3 mischievous raccoons looking for food and the horse carrying most of his supplies broke free and ran back in the direction of the castle never to be seen again. Then during a great storm, a mud slide carried the prince off into a river where he lost the rest of his supplies and barely escaped with his life. On other occasions when he had captured food for much needed nourishment it was quickly taken away by large eagles from the mountain peaks that were surrounding him. Some of the birds where large enough to take the prince off of the cliffs he climbed but seemed to be at peace with only flying away with his game. During one attack after the eagles flew away with his food, he threw stones into the sky hoping to frighten them away from his campsite but accidently brought down a hornet's nest at his feet. The stings were severe, and his body became so greatly swollen that travel was unthinkable and he barely recovered from the incident with his life.

Months had gone by and Drac had plenty of time to think about how he had treated others in his father's kingdom. The raging Bull found in this young man's heart was now losing its great strength due to all his horrific misfortunes. The prince was wet, cold, starving in an unknown land and fearful of every mile he traveled. This was exactly what his heart needed for now he could understand how good his life had truly been. Although being humbled by his position he wasn't ready to fulfill his father's request. That night with tears in his eyes at his campsite while being attacked by every blood sucking insect and parasite known to man he prayed. "Father what I have become is more than I could have ever imagined.

I don't even know when I took this turn for self. I'm ashamed of what I've become and if you can make anything out of me, I'm yours". Sadly, what Drac didn't realize that when he lost his mother, he so focused on keeping himself healthy that he never went back to thinking of the pain of others. The pain and loss were so great it was all the young prince could see, he had become so protective of his heart that he would not allow it to suffer again or to love. Oddly enough after that prayer the insects attacked more than they had before as if they were waiting for his attention. The prince lowered his head as tears continued to slowly run down his face and he then said to himself "I wouldn't have answered my prayer either." With his pain increasing from the bites of these 6-legged little pests his hope began to die.

He then raised his head from his hands to look at this one little terror that had bitten into his arm again. The prince was not fast enough to kill this one specific parasite, so the creature kept coming back for more. Drac again raised his hand to strike hoping to kill this pest but was startled by a black flash that zipped right by his face. He thought to himself "I must be close to passing out from the lack of blood; apparently I'm now seeing black flashes." Then again, this time the black flash zipped right by the campfire, he noticed the parasite flying near his arm was gone. Before he knew it the constant presence of the black flash would almost darken the campfire. Drac's problems of being a midnight snack had somehow been solved by this black flash. He looked up toward the trees searching for a hawk, an eagle or an owl, where could this great winged creature be. Then he noticed the smallest bat that he had ever seen sitting on a branch at the edge of his campsite. "No, this little one can't be my protector" he said to himself, so he kept on looking and looking. At that moment another 6-legged pest decided to go in and feed off the prince. Once again, the black flash zipped by Drac's face, this time though the prince looked right towards the little bat. As he looked closer, he noticed 3 little legs of the insect sticking out of the tiny one's mouth. Then he saw the little one blink 3 times very quickly and with a gulp the legs were gone. The prince was amazed at the speed of the little bat; he had never seen anything like it in all his life. He looked towards his tiny winged avenger and said, "You're extremely fast; I've never seen anything zip in and out as quickly as you did my little friend". The bat became calm almost living off every word Drac spoke to him. "Your constant zipping in and out tonight has saved me from the pain and discomfort of my attackers little one. Zip, I like that name, that's what I'll call you, if that's alright?" At that moment the little bat flew to a branch only a few feet from Drac. Before long Zip would be eating from the princes' hand. Zip was an incredible little creature to say the least, so very small but with his lightning quick speed nothing could outrun or out fly him. Because of his size no other bats saw Zip as an equal or for that matter as one of their kind. This little bat had lived his life all alone making the most out of every day. But for whatever reason Zip was drawn to Drac's voice and became fascinated by his new master. Admiring the little bat, Drac tapped on the area up under his neck and said, "Little one, come closer it's safe" Zip then flew up under his new master's chin to get warm and sleep for the night. Drac was happily surprised that the little creature trusted him so quickly.

With his new friend hope was beginning to heal the heart of the prince. Drac started looking forward to nightfall; Zip was just great entertainment to watch around the campfire. The prince watched amazed at his speed and the little one's great appetite; he seemed never to get full. But once the night sky was clear of pest the small bat would fly up under Drac's chin and get very cozy. Drac's heart had grown very tender due to all the suffering he'd endured and was humbled that such a small little creature could bring him so much joy. As he looked down towards Zip, he said to himself "What is this power you have over me little one, I have a love for you as if you were my very own child." He was saddened for a moment when he thought about how he could not have seen any strength in this little bat if it had not been for all the suffering he had endured. Then he said to himself "What else have I not been able to see due to my own pride, what other precious things have I so easily cast away as useless and unworthy. Was I so blinded by my own gifts that I couldn't see the gifts of others"? He then looked over at little Zip as he slept and said in a whisper "Thank God little one that now I can see".

For whatever reasons the mountain eagles began to stop terrorizing the young prince as if to say they approved of his treatment of the little one. Drac began to gain his strength back now that his game wasn't being stolen from the large creatures. He began to leave some of his food out for the great eagles in his thankfulness and with an eagles screech they repaid his actions by locating prey for the prince. Before long Drac was receiving most of his meals from these great hunters and was sadden when he traveled out of their territory. He was becoming more grateful for his gifts and not seeing it as something to flaunt over others. He knew that Zip was an answer to prayer, so he once again thought of his father's request. The next day he asked his new little friend if he wanted to join him on his quest. Zip blinked several times very quickly giving the prince all his attention. "My father has instructed me to train a small village so that these farmers will be able to protect themselves, what do you think about it?" Zip hoped to meet others like his new master, so he began to do circles in the air showing his excitement. Then Zip headed towards Drac's face and began to do donuts. Drac then said in a whisper "I'll take that as a yes". The days did not seem to be as long with his new little friend. Zip would sleep by day inside one of the carrying cases Drac was able to salvage from the mudslide. When Drac needed to catch game, he would climb the tallest tree and secure his little friend for safety. So, the prince by day became the protector for his new little companion and during the night Zip would return the favor at their campsite. Although at one point feeling somewhat shipwrecked Drac continued the quest his father wanted him to complete because he now felt nothing could be gained by looking back. Zip and the prince had traveled for some distance since leaving the great eagles and were finding it harder and harder to locate food and water. The enemy of his soul began putting thoughts of doubt back into his mind of the great failure he had become. Fatigued from dehydration was setting in due to days without water; he would have to fight to keep his hope alive.

T hen from a mountain peak he could see the village below and thought to himself "At last we should be able to regain our strength, there should be plenty of food and water". As he surveyed the unknown territory, he saw a valley that led straight into the village. Then with great joy he saw a well just outside the village, so he began to head towards it.

He called for zip since it was dusk "Zip, see that tree near the well fly there and stay until I'm sure that it's safe." Zip was practically on the branch before Drac had raised his head from talking to the little one. Drac had no bucket to get the water out of the well so he watched and waited for someone to arrive. Then walking up a small hill next to the well his eyes gazed on something so beautiful and peaceful, something that he hadn't seen in all his life. He saw a young woman coming towards the well with a walking stick, she looked as if she knew every answer to every question that the world would ever ask. There was a peace about her that the prince found to be very captivating. He approached her, at first, she was startled. Then Drac said, "I mean you no harm, I'm only wishing to drink from this well. My name is Drac, what is yours". She said, "my name is Kaitlyna". Kaitlyna, what a beautiful name Drac thought to himself. He then said "I'm the prince of Hungary" with a prideful look on his face that usually made every woman swoon with emotion. He just knew that his pedigree and handsome looks would sweep this commoner off her feet. But Kaitlyna was something very special and noticing the tone of his voice she then replied, "oh my your quite in love with yourself aren't you." Devastated Drac replied "wha… wha…what do you mean" as his voice crackled in humility. She then smiled and said, "Your voice has changed from before; I think there's still hope for you yet." This made the prince smile in relief. Drac had never found himself with someone so completely lovely. As they talked, he found out that she had been born without her sight; his looks would not benefit him during their interaction. He had been so captivated by her beauty that he hadn't noticed how she was using the stick to stay in the path towards the well. The prince stood in amazement that someone who had been given such an unfair start in life could be full of so much joy. Drac surprisingly was at peace that his looks had no value to their interaction, for the first time in many years he simply relaxed and spoke with no impure intentions. Throughout the day Drac and Kaitlyna continued to talk and were both beginning to feel that this was no accidental meeting. Kaitlyna was so intrigued with their conversation she simply became unaware of the time. Suddenly they were startled by the intense roar of a horn being blown from within the village. Fear flooded the face of Kaitlyna as she said, "I must go, Bearook's men count us at this time every day, if I'm not there my family will be, I must go now." "Wait, when can I see you again" Drac shouted. But Kaitlyna was already moving swiftly back towards the village using her stick to guide her on the worn-down path that led from the well he had seen her on earlier. Zip had been on a branch watching his master's interaction for some time, so he flew down landing lightly on the prince's shoulder and gave him a smile with a look of approval towards the beautiful Kaitlyna.

D rac then said, "Zip my little friend
       please go after her, sit atop the house
she is near, and I'll find you, I must see her
again!" Drac turned towards the village and
wondered what could have brought so much
fear to Kaitlyna. Zip did just as his master
asked and was found sitting on a house towards the middle of
the community. Drac quietly climbed up to the roof of the home
where Zip had landed and slowly moved towards the edge to see
what was taking place below. There he could see the town's folk
being lined up as three rough looking savages walked up and down
the line screaming insults and warnings of great punishment to
those that didn't obey. These were Bearook's men, Bearook was
known throughout the land as a wicked warlord feeding on the
innocents of others. These savages attacked the village some
months earlier and did so without any mercy. Any town or village
he found was left with horrors due to his hunger for power that
had no limits. The village did whatever these men commanded to
keep their loved ones from harm. The three savages were left to
tax the people and take anything that pleased them. Drac stayed
out of sight to see what would happen next. But it wouldn't take
long before his blood began to boil from anger. The three began to
question Kaitlyna "what took you so long peasant!" they screamed
while the smell of an unkept mouth and splash of spit flew towards
her face. Then another one said, "She needs to be taught a lesson
and I'll enjoy being the one to teach her." As he grabbed her arm

she screamed "you're hurting me, please have mercy, I'll never be late again" Then the one holding her said as he chuckled "Mercy, you won't find that in the camp of Bearook, Mercy is for those that are not strong enough to take what they want". The prince had great compassion for Kaitlyna and could feel his heart pumping as if it were about to explode. So, before another harsh word could be spoken towards her, he leaped off the roof like a tiger kicking the savage who held Kaitlyna's arm between the eyes leaving him lifeless. The two savages left then grabbed Kaitlyna but would only have their hands on her for a few seconds longer. Before these wicked men could even reach for their weapons, they found themselves lying face down in the mud. One savage slowly pushed himself back up to charge Drac in a rage, but the steel blade found in the hand of the prince would be his end. These men would be no match for the skills of Drac and his experience on the battlefield. But now he also had a raging fire burning from within him to free this village from these evil doers. The last remaining savage came screaming in from behind which gave Drac his position, so he turned quickly and said "O be quiet" right before catching the savage under the chin with the butt of the handle of his blade. The savage was dazed from the blow and began to spit out 3 of his remaining 14 teeth. Once he was able to focus clearly again, he looked towards his wicked brothers in arms and thought this could be my fate today as well. He began to run as if his life depended on it, stopping at the edge of town and looked back towards Drac. Spitting blood on the ground he screamed "you will suffer greatly for what you have done, Bearook will destroy you All!"

The savage lost his attention for just a moment when he saw the little bat sitting on the roof above Drac. Zip had extended his wings as far as he could with an open mouth showing his fangs as his eyes were held wide open trying his best to look as menacing as possible.

T he savage shook his head in disbelief and then turned laughing hysterically and started running towards the wilderness. He had no intentions of going and telling Bearook what had taken place because he knew it would cost him his life. Bearook had no room in his heart for what he considered as weakness; failure was something he chose not to tolerate.

The town's folk were extremely grateful that today they were freed from these wicked men. Drac went over to Kaitlyna and asked if she was alright as he grabbed her hand, she felt his peace and began to breathe softly. She then said "Yes, thank you for saving my life and freeing our village. These men were very wicked but Bearook will come back to destroy us all". Drac thought to himself "Ok father what have you gotten me into, the villagers will never be able to defeat men like these." Then he looked back towards Kaitlyna and said to himself with the biggest smile "But I can't think of a better place to be right now." Zip was still overhead putting on his best intimidating performance as the prince called to him "Easy dragon, he's gone." at that moment Zip flew to the shoulder of the prince as he rubbed the little bat's head. Then one of the villagers began to scream "The young warrior has defeated these wicked men, were saved" At that moment the entire village began to cheer as the look of concern could still be seen on Kaitlyna's face.

Many days had gone by since Drac freed the village and he

was spending every moment he could with the beautiful Kaitlyna. Drac had the approval of the Inn keeper to stay with him until he chose to travel back to his father's castle. These two young souls continued to grow in great fondness of one another. One evening they walked to a clearing in the mountains that stood above the well where they first met. They sat there as zip ate from the hand of Kaitlyna and talked throughout the night. "I've never met anyone like you, there's a peace you have that's undeniable" Drac said. She then replied "As a young girl I suffered much pain and I still have my problems from time to time. But I trust that my Lord will take care of me and that trust has grown through times of great distress. I believe that if you humble your heart to the King of Kings you too can find that peace." At that moment Drac lowered his head in what looked like great despair. Kaitlyna could feel that something was wrong and said, "I hope I did not offend you." Drac then said "No Kaitlyna I could never be offended by any word that would fall from your lips, but you see I do know the Lord." She then said, "what do you mean?" Drac then replied "as a child I lost my mother and rebelled due to the great pain I was under. The years went on and my Father tried his best to intervene, but I continued my path of destruction. The anger and hate I had was consuming me and taking over every part of my body. Then one night after I had given my demons their fill at the local tavern I wished, no I prayed for life to end as I had known it. I was so sorry for all the pain I had caused my father and wanted to be a better son, but I didn't know how to change, or I just didn't have the power too. That night I stood on a great bridge near our castle and thought how better my father would be without me due to the complete terror I had become. The darkness, the emptiness of my soul I was just tired of living with the weight of it all.

But then it happened, I had heard of men speak of great brokenness before given peace that words could not express. The God of the universe spoke to my heart, love like I have never known filled my soul and I heard him say I will do a great work in you. I felt such Joy and peace; I knew I would never be the same again. From that day on I dedicated my life to the Lord, I would give him only my very best. I became the greatest fighter in our kingdom and took great pride in serving our people. This went on for years, I don't know how it happened, but Pride snuck into my heart and began to grow. Perhaps it was time for God to show me what had been there the whole time. I served my Lord in the beginning from a grateful heart but then as time went on, I began to feel different. I had no respect for those that I felt were not giving everything they had to the Lord. I was harsh and critical to all those who served my father. I became a keeper of the law, no mercy would I give to anyone I felt was not giving their all to the lord. It started off so beautiful I gave nothing; I just received this great gift of grace. Later I forgot the meaning of grace, I expected everyone to hold true to my convictions. I was blind to where others may be on their journey of faith thinking they should keep in step with me. That night on the bridge I became very aware of the deep love God has for me, but I never understood the great love he has for others as well. It took my father removing me from the castle to see the prideful man I had become. It wasn't until my loving father sent me on this quest that everything came crashing down around me. I began to see how I benefited off such a gracious father and the good people of the village as I suffered on this journey traveling in fear of death from night to night living in hunger and stripped of all my pride. Everything was taken away, my courage, joy, hope and any presence of peace was removed, at times I shook like a small child in the night wondering if my light was about to be extinguished. Out there in the wilderness as I was being broken God gave me a vision, he showed me my heart from the time he first began working in my life. He showed me that my heart had been cleansed and was washed as white as snow. He showed me that any time I took pride in the things he gave me without thanking him first for his gift a very small place in my heart began to darken. Any of my actions that were a blessing to others made me even more prideful because I did not thank the father who had first given me the gift. My good deeds continued because I had a never-ending passion for pleasing the Lord. But without even knowing it I began performing to earn his love which made me hateful and cruel to others. The worse I felt, the more I pushed myself even harder to be worthy of his gift. I never saw myself as a true son that he would want to bless. But he showed me that over the years my heart had become completely black from my pride with so many words of praise feeding my soul from those around me. I had become puffed up by my knowledge of scripture and could only see the specks in other eyes and not the plank in my own." Drac then began to shake as tears fell from his eyes as Kaitlyna grabbed his hand and held it tightly. Drac then said, "It was then time for God's great discipline, I don't have the words to describe the horrors I went through as I came to your village. One night I even asked the Lord if he was killing me due to the evil spirits that were torturing my mind; I went without sleep for weeks due to my night terrors.

Βut then as I was suffering, I heard that beautiful still small voice in my heart say, "No I'm not killing you; I'm purging you to get rid of anything that doesn't look like my son." God showed me so many strengths in others that I hadn't seen before and that my good deeds were filthy rags compared to what his son did on the cross. What I have learned is this you can take the vilest of men, give them great wealth, health and position, to others and themselves they will look righteous. But remove any of them and watch the foundation start to shake, remove them all and without the light they will find complete destruction. Sometimes we become so foolish that it takes great suffering to bring us back to our loving Father. So Kaitlyna I have had the peace you speak of and I hope that the spirit will fill my soul with that joy again. God is healing me day by day and I am thankful because I want to learn this lesson more than anything else. I do not want to find myself under his loving correction again. I started to feel God's presence again and his healing the night I found little Zip here" As Zip heard his master speak you could see his chest push out with pride and a little smirk of a smile found on his face. Drac once more continued "But then Kaitlyna I saw you walking towards the well where your beauty quenched my thirst, you were an answer to a prayer that I never asked. I knew that after spending time with you that you would be everything that I would ever want." With a great smile on her face and tears running down her cheek she grabbed Drac's hand and said "Yes, we can easily become so foolish and full of ourselves that we go our own ways, we always seem to wonder but we have a great Shepherd who will never forsake us. But don't you be so hard on yourself, I've just been more bless than you Drac." "How's that?" the prince replied in great amazement. She then said with a smile "I would probably get lost much more often if I could see." Drac smiled and shook his head he knew Kaitlyna was just trying to make him feel better. Zip who had been eating from Kaitlyna's hand looked up towards Drac; he now had an expression of sadness knowing that the prince had to suffer greatly to gain a better understanding of God's great mercy.

As the days turned into weeks, they grew closer together and Drac felt it was time to ask Kaitlyna for her hand in marriage. Kaitlyna with a peace in her heart and a love that had continued to grow from their first meeting at the well said "yes". The whole village was excited about the wedding and began to plan for what would be the greatest festival that the village had ever seen. The prince was training those that wanted to become skilled fighters by day while he stayed at the village. What the villagers didn't know was that the first attack was but a few of Bearook's men. The next time he would be bringing his full arsenal of wicked savages to leave nothing standing. Drac simply thought by the information given to him that they should be able to handle the situation due to the size that came before.

After a full day's work Drac could be found at the town's inn with Kaitlyna and Zip where everyone retired to share a meal and fellowship. These nights were most entertaining for Drac and Zip due to the hearty amounts of folklore and legend that these villagers were spinning with great passion. The stories were like none they had ever heard.

One was of a troll that would try to sneak in at night to take food, but his foul odor and its constant hiccups gave him up miles from the village. Another was that of a sinister looking creature from the swamp that would be seen if men took too much from the land without giving it time to heal. They said the creature's breathing sounded like that of a large frog croaking for its next meal. The beast was said to be so intimidating that the villagers restricted anyone from going near the swamp. Of course, this made every young person even more curious until the sounds of the frogs croaking could be heard coming from the swamp, that usually brought them quickly back to the safety of the village. The Inn keeper swore with an expression of fear his father's story. His father told him of the time he had to travel far away to a city for medicine and while coming back he was attacked by four wicked thieves. He was running for his life along the marshes but the four were closing in on him. He couldn't outrun the wicked savages, so he went further into the swamp hoping to lose them and double back. The savages were just as cunning and soon had him surrounded. My father said the men began to chuckle as they thought about all the horrible things they were about to do to him. But then as they stood there in waist high water everything became very quiet "do you hear that, what's that wicked noise?" One of the savage's said. My father heard it as well and found the noise to be incredibly frightening and thought

"I'm surrounded by these wicked savages and now with this horrible croaking, what terrible fate awaits me?" Then Whoosh, suddenly at that moment the four robbers were taken under the marsh simultaneously as my father stood paralyzed with fear. He was terrified at what he had just witnessed and made no effort to move hoping not to be the next one to disappear. He stayed lifeless for some time then realized he could not stand there any longer, so he began in the direction of his wagon being very careful not to disturb the marsh. But as he started, he could hear the sinister croaking again, this time he could tell that the noise was directly behind him. He began to turn very slowly gritting his teeth together, hoping his fate would not be the same as the thieves. My father's eyes became widened more than they had ever been before as he stood there with this swamp creature. The creature's webbed like skin was colored in green and black; it stood about six foot seven. He had never seen anything like it, the two of them stood there staring at each other. The creature then raised his right leg out of the water and began to scratch the back of his own head with it; he scratched and scratched then extended out both of his arms as if he needed to rest. Once the creature lowered his arms it croaked three times towards my father then turned and went back into the marsh. As my father watched the creature leave in the opposite direction, he saw no reason to stand still any longer. Moving quickly, he headed out of the swamp, then he began running as he remembered the frightful head of the creature. My father never traveled by the marsh ever again. As the inn keeper finished his story one of the other villager's began laughing "He,he,he,heeee, Hank you still telling everyone about that over grown tadpole" Which the Inn keeper responded, "Charlie my father saw, what my father saw, no matter if you believe it or not!"

Charlie responded, "I would like to catch it though; I bet it would taste like chicken." Everyone chuckled as the two continued to banter back and forth over their tall tales.

Many others told of Goblins, Monsters and creatures that were said to be found throughout the land near the village. Drac also heard of how Bearook and his men ravaged their community by first hearing a great horn blown from the hillside before they attacked. This continued every evening and the prince with Kaitlyna enjoyed all the tall tales that were told while Zip ate from his master's hand. There was one legend though more than any other that was being told night after night by the villagers, a story of a great black dragon. Their eyes would widen as they told the stories of the beast and you could hear their excitement with each word spoken. They said that this creature had not been seen in some time. But that at dusk during different seasons this black dragon could be seen flying throughout the sky larger than one of their homes. This made the village children very leery of going out after sundown. At that time one of the elders began telling his Great grandfather's story of the black dragon. He said that the village many generations ago was being invaded by 3 red fire breathing dragons. The strongest and bravest of their men were no match for these creatures. For many weeks they were trapped inside the caves as their crops were being destroyed and hope began to die in the hearts of those remaining. The despair grew so great that some prayed for their very lives to be taken, others as the starving continued began to turn on one another. The caves deep in the mountains were their only place of protection from these hungry creatures but if the attacks continued these caves would also become their graves. Then on a night that seemed no different than any other it happened; the sky began to turn black, darker than any night they had ever seen. The black dragon was at his strongest when the sky was void of any light. While the villagers were hiding in the caves from the dragons it felt as if the world above them was beginning to shake. They could hear what sounded like a raging war coming from heaven, as if the mountains were crashing into one another above their very heads. The old man said his Great grandfather's curiosity got the best of him, so he moved towards the edge of the cave to see what was taking place. He could see the 3 dragons breathing fire in all directions as if they knew not where their adversary was coming from. He then saw the first dragon fall from the sky, a little while later the second, a massive beast like scream could be heard throughout the caves then he saw the third crash through one of their tool sheds. When the old man looked up for just a split second, he could see the great black dragon flying as the moon came through the darkness and then it was gone. He said they went out to inspect each of the dragons and saw the marks on the first one's flesh. One's head was crushed by the great pressure of the black dragon's talons. Another found without any battle wounds had an expression unlike the others as if he had been in a trance before he had hit the ground with his eyes still opened.

The third and last dragon was the largest of them all; this beast had both of his wings broken in half. But the wounds were very odd they were found at the same distance on each wing as if the black dragon had hit him from behind breaking them at the same time. This would have made the villager's savior larger than anything they could have ever imagined. Many of their stories about the black dragon seemed to come at times of great suffering. Drac thoroughly enjoyed listening to tales about the black dragon more than any other story but thought to himself these are only fables told by good simple town folk, nothing more.

While the planning and preparing for the wedding continued, Drac could not stop thinking about the expression from the one savage that fled into the wilderness. He thought to himself, could we be wrong about the size of this wicked army should we begin to move this entire town back to Hungary within my father's protection. He then shook his head for tomorrow would be his wedding day, he only wished that both his mother and father could have been with him.

The next day the two were face to face while everyone in the village watched the two young lovers share their vows on never forsaking one another through all the seasons good or bad. Everything was perfect for the two but as they moved in closer to continue the ceremony the village was startled by a loud horn coming from the hillside. Everyone turned and looked towards the hills below the mountain peaks and Drac said "No it cannot be, the savage has returned." But the horn blew again, this time louder than before. Drac was in disbelief as far as the eye could see stood warriors, hundreds of warriors that looked ready for battle. The village in just a moment turned from joy to horror. Men on horseback began to move towards the town. Drac with only farmers and townsfolk moved into positions of protection for their loved ones. Then a flag was raised high above these warriors, Drac began to scream out instructions for those not fit for battle to run towards the caves. He did not recognize the symbol that flew overhead at first but then he thought to himself "No it cannot be, The Fire of the Dragon, it's my father". He was right; it was the king with his strongest company of troops. It was quite the sight to see these warriors coming towards the village. The town's people were amazed at the armor and size of the men that were moving towards them, it was very impressive to say the least. Then Drac screamed "Father is that really you" With a smile as big as the black dragon; the King came off his horse and embraced his only son for what seemed like an eternity. The King had sent some of his best scouts to follow the prince on his quest and report by messenger hawk while his troops were waiting. Once the king found out the prince had started moving in the direction of the village, he began his own quest of protection. The King then told his son of his plans to keep his beloved tracked and that he had no intention of leaving him alone, even if it felt like it to Drac. He gave Drac the bad news that Bearook's army had turned and were heading back towards the village. The King told the villagers that by his information the savages were maybe a month away from reaching them. He then invited them to come and live in Hungary.

"In Hungary" the King said, "your families will be protected by a much stronger force and there is plenty of land for future generations to prosper." The entire town confused and frightened agreed that leaving would be best based on what they had witnessed before.

The King's kindness quickly made everyone in the village feel that they were already apart of Hungary. He then loudly declared "But first there needs to be a wedding." The King sent for his personal chefs so that there would be food prepared for this village that they had never tasted or experienced. The King wanted this night to be something his son and future daughter in law would never forget.

That night as the great celebration continued the King held his son tight and said, "Yes there it is, I can see it in your eyes, I have my son back." The overjoyed King then pulled Kaitlyna over for a bear hug she would never forget and was amazed at his son's new little friend. The King listened intently as Drac explained how Zip came into his life after much suffering and how the little one was so incredibly gifted. The King looked down at Zip and said, "little one you truly are a gift from God". Zip swelled up with pride as he heard the King's words then flew into his beard for comfort. At this everyone began to laugh uncontrollably as the night couldn't have been any better. The celebration went on until the wee hours of the morning but the plans for evacuating the village would begin at daybreak.

Everyone worked towards one common goal which was leaving before Bearook's forces returned. The King knew his horses and men needed as much rest as possible in case there was combat on the way home. Days later the village and the Kings forces would be ready to travel to Hungary. Everything precious had been put onto a wagon with a skilled driver holding the reins of a well-rested steed ready for the journey. The King mounted his horse then yelled with excitement "Well then let's head home." Many of the villagers began to cheer with great anticipation in the future there were hoping for.

Suddenly a loud horn blew that shook everyone to their core, a more sinister sounding horn than before and then throughout the land there blew hundreds more. The horns made such a deep wicked sounding noise that it became somewhat maddening to everyone in the village. Then there he was, the wicked Bearook, with a laugh that could be heard as loud as the horn itself.

The King could not understand how his reports were incorrect. He was unaware that one of his last scouts had been taken captive and Bearook had been giving the hawk false information. Bearook's men were great in number but the Kings men were as skillful as you would ever find. Drac then said to Kaitlyna, "Take Zip and your family to the caves and wait for me to come and get you.

Bearook had traveled a very long distance; he saw no need to send his entire army down to attack the village. If anything, it would be entertaining to just send a small group since they still greatly outnumbered the King's army. Bearook then thought to himself "Yes, this could be very helpful in watching their technique, I've heard of the great skill that the Fire of the Dragon possesses." The savage then screamed "triple the troops and destroy them all, makes no mind to me if you bring me the King or his sons head first." As the battle began; Bearook became furious as he witnessed the skill of the small army that was defeating his men so quickly. He ordered for the horn to be blown so what was left of his men would return to camp. As Bearook's men were running back up the hillside he gave the command for his archers to rain arrows down on them. Their failure to defeat a much smaller force would not be tolerated. He then screamed towards his remaining army "Tomorrow or any other day I will not allow failure, if so, you will pay with your lives". The prince and everyone there were in shock by the cold and callous actions that had just taken place. Drac said to himself "Yes this one is far more wicked than I have ever seen, he must be stopped." Drac had led his father's men with honor in defeating Bearook's savages and the King beamed with pride seeing the valor of his son. Drac's heart had become heavy, he knew they were completely outnumbered but wanted to feed their hearts with hope instead of despair, to show courage instead of fear so he said, "I'm amazed at what I've seen today, what courage and fire, villagers who look more like lions than farmers." Then he scanned back and forth at the men he had fought with so many times before. He looked down towards the ground as if he didn't deserve their loyalty, the men were silent as Drac slowly raised his head and then he said "I am humbled that God would give me such a great army to fight alongside, A Great Dragon's Fire you are, but you are also my brothers of Hungary." He then bowed his head in honor to show his great respect to them all. The army was puzzled, it was Drac on the battlefield some would say he never looked better, but the men were not used to the meekness of his speech. As the army thought about the words and manner from which Drac's words were spoken they all turned towards Bearook and in unisons began chanting their battle cry. The King could not have been prouder of his son as he began walking over to him. The two embraced grateful to be left standing after the first attack. The King said, "I love you my son" Drac replied "As I do you father."

Bearook was watching from the hill and quickly became disgusted by what was taking place and said "O my, their having a moment, they need to be reminded that death has come for them all, bring me my crossbow and one of my poisoned arrows. Great fear will soon overtake these simple fools and their rejoicing will cease once this deadly tip finds its unknowing victim." He then raised his crossbow and shot the arrow with an arch towards the village; it flew rapidly until it hit an opening of a warrior's suit of armor. The arrow finding the one area not protected would be this man's downfall. The King still embracing his son could now feel Drac's body beginning to weaken. The King began to scream "What's wrong my son, Drac what's wrong." as the prince fell from his arms. The arrow had found its way to the Kings only son.

At that moment in the cave Kaitlyna and Zip knew something was terribly wrong, they fled towards the village. Sadly, their greatest fears would come true. Her Drac would now be laying facedown without the light she so felt from him. She screamed his name, turned him over and while tears flowed from her face she cried "How can this be, you were my gift from God, I don't understand." The King standing over his son had not moved since he fell from his arms. He saw the arrow and was in shock, "This makes no sense, such a small opening to hit, he is almost completely covered, Lord how can this be, my son, my only son!" he said. He then fell to his knees alongside Kaitlyna were they both wept over the prince.

Great fear gripped the entire village as they saw what one rogue arrow did to their great champion. Bearook was amazed and began to laugh hysterically, soon his army joined in his laughter. As he caught his breath he proclaimed "In all my days I've never seen my God's give me such a gift, your redeemer is dead. Please, you have no time to pity him for tomorrow you will all find the same fate." The laughter went on for some time then Bearook ordered his savages to make camp. The wicked tyrant could have easily moved his entire army in that night but wanted the village to grow in sorrow and fear before he took it. He would be sending his entire force the next day, a monstrous and vile group to destroy everything in his path. There would be nothing left standing after he attacked, the foul barbarian wanted victory and it would come at any cost. At that moment there seemed to be no hope for anyone in the village, everyone had been sure that Drac was an answer to prayer. But now they saw the Kings son lifeless from what seemed like an unfortunate event or even worse the hand of God. Sadly, what the King didn't know was that the numbers of Bearook's men were so great that even if Drac had survived they all would still be destroyed. Bearook continued to laugh as he raised his axe towards his heartless brutes and screamed "Hungary's great Dragon has been destroyed by a Devil." At that moment every weapon was lifted in the air as Bearook's men began to chant his name. Bearook then screamed "Rest for tomorrow I will have all of their heads or the heads of those who fail me." as an evil sneer could be seen growing upon his face. He continued to laugh as he walked towards his tent screaming "Tomorrow, tomorrow little village I will bring you much sorrow."

Back at the village fear and despair continued to grow in the hearts of everyone. Poor little Zip could not comprehend what had happen to the prince; he continued to watch him and wondered why he just didn't get up. But as he waited and watched he remembered other creatures that had seemed frozen in life during his travels. Different animals he came upon in his life that were perfectly still as Drac now lay with no movement. Then it hit him like the others his master will never wake up again in this world. His relationship with Drac was something he had never experienced. Even with his own kind he felt like an outsider due to being so little. Zip thought of the first night he met the prince and smiled while tears began to fill his little eyes. He knew that their encounter was something very special; something that he had never known in his entire life. Their friendship for the brief time they knew each other had become very precious to the little bat.

As he continued to look down at the lifeless body of his master from the roof of one of the homes in the village, Zip could see the suffering of those that befriended his master surrounding him. He saw the King, Kaitlyna and all the towns folk in great despair. Thoughts began running into his mind, I wish there was something I could do, something to help, but I'm so little. There is nothing I can do to bring back my master, nothing to stop all this pain, nothing to stop the horrors that will come for them all tomorrow. There is nothing that I can do to change the storm that's coming for them. But then hope began to grow in his little heart, he thought to himself yes there is nothing I can do but I know of one who can, I'll go to the Black Dragon.

He then began to smile because Zip knew there was no such thing as the Black Dragon. Something much greater than a Black Dragon, a bat but just not any bat, an ancient bat, the father of all bats. This King of night winged creatures had a wingspan that of 3 times the size of any known dragon ever to be found. The ancient bat also had the speed and strength ten times that of any known creature. But what made the beast so deadly was he could attack his prey in pitch black due to his sonar. The sound waves gave this creature every move his enemy would make. Any predator wishing to go against the King of bats had no chance of victory. The great bat also possessed a power, an ancient power that had grown within him from the dawn of time. So, Zip thought to himself "I'll go to the King" even though this would be an extremely frightful thing for him to do. For no one had ever gone to the King's lair. The fear of his great strength and his mysterious powers were enough to keep any of the mightiest creatures away. But Zip's love for his master was greater than his fear of what might happen to him. Zip knew where the Kings lair was located but also knew how heavily protected the entrance and surrounding territory would be. High atop the side of a great mountain there would be a cave on a cliff where no human could travel. But his love for the prince was far more powerful than his fear. As Zip's determination grew, he began to fly with incredible speed towards the great winged leviathan's lair. As he flew near the mountain peak the Kings mighty protectors became aware of his presence and started to move aggressively towards the little bat. Massive bats, creatures of terror came out to turn little Zip away. Zip communicated to these monstrous creatures that he had urgent business with the great bat. They all in unison began to scream in a great pitch that drove Zip back against the rocks of the cliff. The creatures could see that Zip was no match for their sonic blast, so they stopped their attack on the little bat. Zip began to dust off the dirt from the rocks that had covered him from the impact and looked up at the massive creatures he could in no way over power. He then took the biggest, deepest breath that he had ever taken before and thought to himself "I'm so afraid, I can't accomplish this on my own." He then heard the smallest voice, a whisper that sounded like it was coming from his heart. It said "fly" at that moment the bat felt a peace come over him that was indescribable. Zip began staring into the eyes of the massive creatures and both of his eyebrows began to raise high up onto his forehead. He then showed his little razor shaped teeth as a small smirk began to rise on his face. Before these monsters knew what had happen dust flew from the side of the rocks near the cliff where Zip had landed.

The bats were simply amazed; it was as if Zip vanished right before their eyes. At first the large bats circled several times trying to see if they could tell what direction Zip flew towards. The massive creatures then turned quickly to fly towards the entrance of the cliff but were stopped when the King communicated to them all, "let the little one come to me". They all bowed at his instruction and flew back to their positions on the mountain peaks.

Zip was now flying at record speeds toward the cave and his meeting with this ancient, winged, Leviathan. As he made his way into the cave his little heart started to beat faster than the speed he was traveling but then, there he was. The great King, no other bat or creature for that matter had ever made their way into his presence. He had the power to see into the heart of any living thing and if unworthy one would collapse and never be heard of again. But the King would soon see that the little bats heart was something very special. He focused intently on the little one and witnessed the horrors of the village as he used his power to search Zip's little soul. He was wonderfully surprised at the care Drac had given the little bat, he was also impressed by the fight and valor he saw in the prince and the love that was given at his passing. The King became saddened and disheartened at the treatment Zip had received from his own kind throughout his life. But was also amazed how one treated so wrongly could have such compassion and love for others. The ancient bat then began to communicate to Zip, to the little bat it sounded like a whisper coming from his heart. "Little one you are more precious than any creature that I've ever seen, I am very pleased to call you one of my children. But I can only bless those creatures that are mine, he is human." At that time tears started to fill Zip's little eyes and his lower lip began to quiver, once again as his head lowered, he thought to himself that now all hope is truly lost. "Little one!" the King continued as Zip looked towards the great beast. "This gift I give will not be for any human, but I give this gift to you. I can see what he has done for you and what he means to you. I'll save Drac, because of the love I have for you little one." At that time Zip started going into a full flurry of a flying frenzy, he would have zipped in and out for ever if it was not for the King getting his attention again. The great bat said "Drac will never be the same after I've given him this gift, after his transformation he will never be fully human, it will be as if he was born again. The prince will become one of us, a creature of supernatural strength but only if his heart is pure enough to except it. If he, at the time of his death, was humble, his body will accept my power but if not, he will remain dead." The Bat King then said to his war commander "assemble all of our forces we leave now for this village." As Zip and the Great Bat began to leave the cave heading towards the village all the bats had lowered their heads in honor. Zip was amazed at how many of his brothers and sisters there were in the caves, thousands and thousands of bats paying their respect to the great Bat King. He then thought how rightfully so that the creatures should be lowering their heads to one that is so easily worthy of their esteem. The Bat King became amused as he could read Zip's thoughts and then communicated this to the little bat "this honor, the honor you see before you little one is not for me, it is all being directed towards you."

Zip in shocked replied "But why" He then explained, "These children of mine are very powerful creatures, they have defeated many wicked adversaries, but they see something in you they lack. You could have been so easily destroyed yet you still came into my lair. They see your faith to move mountains and your love for others more than yourself something they lack. They mistakenly know they look to their own strength unlike you who righty came to the father in your weakness. Little one they wish to be like you more than you'll ever know." Zip was amazed that these massive beasts were paying their respects to him, he was overwhelmed and felt unworthy of such a great gift. The Bat King then told Zip "It's time little one, we must now leave."

Back at the village the tears of loss had removed any hope and exhausted everyone completely. Drac's body had been taken and was put in one of the rooms of Kaitlyna's home. Kaitlyna and her father in law were at the dinner table giving each other words of comfort. The King in such great despair started to blame himself "I should have never sent him alone, I could have been a better father, Drac's death is my fault" as a river of tears once more ran down his face. Kaitlyna also under great suffering took the hand of the King and said "This is not your doing; we cannot make any sense of this but it's not your fault. If you had not sent him, we here in this village would have had no chance of freedom. No one knew the size of Bearook's army and that arrow, who could have known it would have hit such a small opening." After speaking she began to weep. The King moved in even closer and put Kaitlyna's head towards his chest and said "We must get everyone to the caves and go as far as they will take us, Bearook will not be able to surround us in the cave and we will fight them off as long as we can. Hopefully there will be an exit on the other side of these caves, or we will make one." As they sat there they both felt something very strong, a cold chill ran through the village and the sky began to turn black, darker than anyone had ever seen. The homes began to shake uncontrollably as the dishes and pictures fell from the walls and cupboards. The villagers and Bearook's army all came out running from their homes and tents to see what was taking place. No one could see their hand in front of their face; the wind blew so hard it put out any fire that was being used for sight. Bearook and his men stood in shock looking down towards the village and waited to see if the earth was about to open and swallow them all.

No one could see, the darkness was totally void of any light. Suddenly Kaitlyna and the King heard a monstrous crash as the great Bat King had broken in through the roof and his massive talons were reaching for the prince. The King ran into the room with his sword raised to protect his son's body and was overwhelmed with shock as he saw the creature. He screamed "let my son go you demon" raising his sword to strike the ancient bat. Zip then flew in towards the Kings face quickly going back and forth in front of his eyes squeaking to get the Kings attention.

But the King screamed "little one stop, the demon is taking my son" Kaitlyna rushed in and placed her hands on the King, saying "Wait, we in this village have been told by our forefathers about an ancient creature that comes in great times of suffering to help the weak, maybe this is that creature." The great Bat then took the prince and placed him on the roof. Zip flew to a higher position to observe both his father and master. Drac's father who feared his son would be food for the great beast stepped back as Kaitlyna pulled him. The Bat King investigated the heart and mind of Drac and saw all the suffering he had to endure so that he could come into full maturity. He could see that he had been healed of his selfish pride and that the pain he endured would keep him meek and always move him towards mercy. The Bat King turned to Zip and communicated "This one will be able to accept my great gift little one." hearing this Zip got all excited flying in circles above Drac. The Bat King then turned back toward the prince and screamed up towards the heavens as if he were summoning a great army or speaking to the creator himself. A great green mist started to pour out from his mouth toward the prince. It was completely covering him; the green mist began to go into every pore of the prince and every cell of his body. The mist lifted Zip's master up from the roof; he floated in midair as the green mist continued to consume every organ of his body. Drac was being changed from the inside out. Kaitlyna and the King of Hungary were speechless as they watched in wonder what the great beast was doing with the green mist. The King was describing to Kaitlyna everything that was taking place as she tightened her hand around his. Dracs father was in awe as he watched his son floating with the great winged beast. Then the King, seeing the great creature in all its glory said, "It's a bat, in all my days I've never seen something as powerful or majestic as this bat, but what is he doing to my son?" Bearook too had been watching as the green mist gave light surrounding the great beast. He thought to himself "This creature is beyond any power I've ever known, if I could control him I would have the power to control others, no one could stop me from conquering this world, yes this creature will do my bidding, or it will die." Suddenly a scream could be heard throughout Bearook's entire camp, the scream brought all his men to their knees. This powerful scream strained the ears of all those savages; this scream was coming from the mouth of Drac Van Der Merwe. Kaitlyna bewildered by what was going on around her cried out as she grabbed Drac's father "What's going on, please tell me what's going on." Drac's father shouted, "It cannot be, with my own eyes it cannot be, my son you're alive, Kaitlyna Drac is alive!" Zip had never moved faster, even faster than when he was with the bat King in the cave. He was overjoyed seeing life come from his master and friend.

Everyone stood in awe as the moon came through the clouds and there it was clearer and more magnificent than ever. The great Bat King extended his wings and those present were stunned at his incredible size. The villagers began to say to one another "It's true, all the stories were true, the creature does exist." The great bat looked down toward the village and saw the King, he slightly nodded his head in respect for he knew of the good deeds his kingdom had accomplished for the weak.

The great bat turned once more towards Drac and communicated this one thought "arise my son, arise". The massive creature began to fly away as he nodded his head towards Zip. The ancient beast flew over Bearook's army as several were knocked over by the massive wind gust, many ran in fear of the monstrous creature but then the bat King was gone. Bearook looked at Drac as he began to rise from the roof, he could see his eyes were glowing with the green mist. He then yelled in anger "You were dead, my arrow killed you, how can this be." Drac looked down at his father and wife; he then calmly said "Tell everyone to go to the cave, everyone, our troops as well father." His father replied, "My son we will not leave you, their numbers are great, you cannot defeat this army alone." "Father" Drac said calmly "I'm not alone, so go quickly." At that moment the King could see bat like teeth growing from the mouth of his son and muscular features building up around his face and body. Then the King quickly began to scream "To the caves, everyone to the caves." Some of the King's bravest spoke up "We cannot leave Drac to fight this army alone my King." At which the King replied, "I don't intend too but for now get everyone to the caves." Drac then jumped off of the roof towards his wife and said as his voice began to change more monstrous "Kaitlyna, my precious Kaitlyna I'm the same man you once knew but now I need you to be safe so please go with my father into the caves, please Kaitlyna go." She replied "Drac, you sound like a monster". She then put her hands towards his face and could feel the massive fangs that had grown from his jaw. " what have you become Drac!" The Prince replied "This is the monster I must become; these savages will show no mercy towards your village. The great Bat has given me the power to control this gift, but these savages will only fear the monster inside me." At that moment Drac's voice became even more fearfully monstrous and said, "please go to the cave!" Kaitlyna in shock with fear said nothing and started to turn towards the cave. Drac's heart grew with compassion for his wife after seeing her tremble in fear, so he said quickly "Kaitlyna." Even though she did not recognize her loved one's voice she still turned back towards Drac and whispered nervously "Yes" He then said in this monstrous voice "Did you know that I'm the prince of Hungary." A joy and peace began to fill her heart she now knew that her Drac was still present. Once more the prince said "please go and be safe" now with a smile and peace in her heart she was led away by Drac's father. Drac screamed as the transformation continued, massive talons grew through his boots and his clothes began to rip due to the expanding monstrous muscle mass. Fingernails like daggers grew from his hands and a rubbery membrane began to take over his body as wings grew from his arms to his hips. Drac had been completely transformed into this monstrous bat like creature. In the next moment his sound waves warned him of an incoming danger, so he quickly turned and caught a poison arrow shot towards his head by Bearook. Drac smiled as the arrow lay flat in his hand; he then began to blow on the arrow, as the green mist flowed from his mouth the arrow wilted away. Drac then looked up and pointed towards his enemies and said in his new voice "I will now come to you and bring you new nightmares." Bearook screamed "By my hand you will fall, my God's will give me your head tonight!" Drac then raised his hand towards the sky as it began to darken even more, Bearook's army watched in amazement as their hearts began to fill with fear.

One screamed "how are we to destroy a creature we can't even see, this is madness". Then another "Bearook has brought this evil on our heads tonight, our sins have found us." Bearook angered by the fear growing in his men ordered them to rain down poisoned arrows toward the village. Thousands upon thousands of arrows were now flying towards Drac, he could hear them all flying in his direction. As he raised his hand towards the arrows and screamed, they froze in midair. The savages were horrified in shock to see the arrows hanging from the sky outlined by what looked like the green mist. Drac then motioned his hand back towards Bearook's camp, in an instant the arrows flew faster than before hitting thousands upon thousands of his men. Drac started moving up the hillside towards Bearook's army, his eyes were glowing from the green mist. Many of the wicked barbarians stood in fear shaking like small children as they watched this monstrous creature moving towards them. Drac allowed the green mist to light up all around him so that his enemies could see the monster that was coming for them. Some thought to themselves "run and fight another day" and others "if we kill Bearook maybe the monster will stop" Even though several had become fearful, the majority were so still full of their own hate and arrogance in their abilities and thought to themselves "I'll be known throughout the land as the one who killed this great beast." They were more concerned about gaining their own glory than leaving this land with their very lives.

Bearook was furious and called for his men to release the wolfs onto Drac. These beasts were very vicious creatures and would tear anything apart that the master commanded them to destroy. Once released you could hear Bearook screaming for these creatures to destroy Drac and leave no one in the village alive. As the wolves ran toward Drac their heavy breathing could be heard from a mile away. These creatures lived their lives in cages and were trained for one thing. That one thing was to create and inflict as much cruelty towards others as they were given. As the wolves got closer to Drac, Bearook could see the green mist expanding and becoming very dense so he began screaming frantically "Prince you coward, there is no place you can hide from the great Bearook, you mangy animals bring me his flesh." Drac could see an uncontrollable amount of drool falling from the wolves as their growling became louder. As they went into the green mist you heard what sounded like a savage attack. It was as if the wolves were tearing Drac apart but then the noise began to die down. An eerie silence fell throughout the hillside and it was unnerving to those watching from the outside. The savages made no noise but stood frozen; puzzled as to why they could not hear the beast tearing the prince apart any longer. Bearook continued to stare at the mist straining to hear something, anything then he screamed "Well then bring me back his head" then slowly the mist started to dissipate, and figures started to emerge. Bearook could hear what sounded like puppies playing with their master. Drac had taken control over the beast and was petting some of their stomachs while the others were jumping up on the prince for attention. As the mist lifted, these wolfs no longer looked malnourished and diseased as if the mist filled every cell and organ healing their body's. Drac then called his new friends in and gave them instructions to protect the children and villagers in the caves.

The beast ran with excitement to please their new master and would never be used by the wicked barbarian Bearook again. The villagers were frightened at first as they watched these monstrous creatures running towards them. They could see the tails wagging so they stood still in hopes that they would not be torn apart. As the wolves came closer, they ran towards the children and began to lick their faces. Laughter from the children could now be heard coming out from the caves.

The savage Bearook became even more enraged but before he could give the command for his entire force to move towards Drac, he noticed the green mist was moving aggressively towards his camp. The great bat had given Drac majority of his powers, so the prince started running towards the camp then with one jump flew over and commanded the green mist to subside. Bearook and his army became enraged that their sight had been taken away again and that this monstrous creature was now above them. They frantically began trying to light their torches but could not due to the wicks being coated by the green mist. Drac was now using sound waves safely above the army below. With another Bat like screech Drac motioned his hand towards the camp of Bearook. The green mist started to flow throughout the entire campsite, Bearook's men were so confused and fearful because of the mist they began to fight among themselves. Being blind in battle they continued to destroy one another, hundreds upon hundreds of Bearook's men were falling by their very own hands. Bearook screamed "have you all gone mad, this beast has you fighting one another." But then the savage being wickedly cunning as a man of war thought if the wicks wont light then I'll burn this camp down to the ground before I'm defeated. He then commanded those not affected by the green mist to burn all the tents of the camp. The fire became so bright that Drac's own eyesight had to readjust due to his sensitivity and this would leave him somewhat vulnerable to any attack. Bearook could now see the bat monster flying above his camp so he quickly commanded those men still of their right minds to aim for the creature. Several arrows had bounced off Drac and could not penetrate any part of his body except for the membrane up underneath the wings. That area from his hip to the wrist could be somewhat vulnerable if attacked with the right weapon. One arrow did find its way into that area of the membrane and Bearook then thought to himself as the fires continued to burn around him "At last this may be the weakness I've been looking for." He then said, "You fool's aim towards the wings with every arrow we have, aim for the wings". Several arrows began to fly into the membrane of Drac's wings as you could hear him scream from the piercing that was taking place. Drac started to move lower to the ground since the arrows were taking some of his energy away. Then Bearook screamed "rope the creatures talons, the feet of the prince, that will bring him down!" Drac was using all his energy to stay above so his healing ceased as Bearook continued to attack. Some of the savages holding the ropes around Drac's talons were now 30 feet off the ground as Bearook screamed "Don't let go or I'll have your heads." The arrows were flying in by the hundreds, so the prince thought it may be better to heal from the ground. So, he quickly flew behind a large rock and allowed the green mist to concentrate all its power on healing him.

Bearook could see that the mist would heal him completely, so he quickly commanded all his savages that were left to move in and slaughter him. The Prince looked like a caged lion as he fought off the savages that were coming for him. It was amazing to watch the prince move with such great speed and agility as he fought off Bearook's men in his monstrous form. Drac's new power was something these wicked savages were not ready for; when hit they flew some 70 feet from where Drac first made contact. Even though the prince was still greatly outnumbered none could strike him at close range. His skills and supernatural strength could not be matched by any of these savages. Bearook enraged screamed "Am I surrounded by foolish children, you idiots can you not see that you are no match for him close range. Move farther out and let your arrows fly once more." Just as Drac was beginning to heal completely and fly as the monstrous bat like creature once more he could feel arrows piercing his flesh. As Drac began to scream Bearook was pleased to see that the arrows were weakening him once more but thought of another way to inflict even more damage from a safe distance. He then commanded his men to go back in with long spears and pierce him like a wild boar. Bearook laughing uncontrollable yelled towards Drac "Prince your about to be gutted like a pig, I think your new bride will need much consoling." With rage Drac screamed once more, the arrows that were in his wings were pushed out with amazing speed and force by the green mist and found their way into several of the savages that were surrounding him as horns could be heard in the background. What Drac had not known was that his father had no intention of letting his son go fight this great army alone.

The King commanded his army to flank Bearook's camp on both sides, he instructed his men not to move into battle unless Drac fell from the sky. The King knew that Bearook would use his men as pawns to stop Drac from defeating his savages. So, he stayed out of sight that was until he saw his son fall from the sky. The troops at that time had started moving in closer to Bearook's camp and when the King could see his son covered in arrows that was enough for him to strike. The King had commanded the horns of Hungary to be blown for that was the sign for his army to light the torches and move in to defeat what was left of Bearook's men. Bearook was now more enraged than ever, he had never tasted defeat and could see it coming closer than he had ever known before. The King's men had fought their way towards Drac and now had surrounded him with a wall of protection. Drac was now healing at a much faster pace because of the men that were shielding him from Bearook's attack. One of the King's men that was protecting Drac screamed as his back was still turned towards the prince "My Lord your father said you may need our help until you gain the knowledge of this new gift you have been given." Drac then said in his monstrous voice "That sounds like my father." Which made the warrior turn to look upon the prince. The warrior became speechless as he looked onto the face of this bat like creature and froze. Drac then said, "Turn quickly before you're wounded." the warrior then snapped out of his trance and did so. Drac said to himself as he shook his head "surely I don't look that bad." Some of the other warriors protecting Drac who had fought with him before and could care less what he looked like started jokingly screaming as they continued to fight off Bearook's men.

"Well your highness you've had better days" Then another said laughing "have you done something different with your hair" Then another "Your father said you were in a season of change, but this is ridiculous." Even as the blades were coming from the savages the men could not stop laughing. Drac then said as he was regaining all his strength in his monstrous voice "Yes gentlemen all of this is quite hilarious but remember one day I may pick you up off the ground as an eagle does its prey." Which then caused all the men to stop laughing, Drac then began to smile as he could feel the fear grow around him. He then said, "Men of Hungary I thank you for your protection and for being my brothers." He then summoned all his power as the green mist began to grow, the men around him were now being healed of any wounds they had suffered and a great strength they had never felt before began to grow in them as well. Then a Bat like screech was heard and Drac flew back into the sky as he said to himself "Use your speed Drac they can't hit a moving target."

The King and Bearook had found one another on the battlefield so the savage charged Drac's father with an evil intent. The King's skill of fighting had been perfected over the decades but Bearook was a beast of a man that was strong unlike the king had ever seen. The King without the strength of his youth fought with every ounce of his being, blocking every blade that was swung at him by Bearook. Each block that was given had the King moving towards the ground as if Bearook was pounding in a spike that was fighting off his master's commands. The weakened King fell to his knees as he no longer had the strength to hold the shield up for protection. Bearook with a wicked and vain expression said with a chuckle "Great King ha, you look more like a child compared to the great Bearook." As the savage swung his sword towards the head of his enemy it was suddenly stopped by a monstrous bat like wing. Enraged Bearook looked up and saw Drac healed and in his terrifying creature like form. Bearook stood paralyzed as he witnessed close up every detail of Drac's monstrous form and his frightfully overwhelming presence. The savage had never seen such an intimidating foe in all his life. He forced himself to move back away from the prince as he saw Drac once more raise his hand to bring total darkness. Bearook could see the expressions in the men's faces as if they pitied him for the life he had lived and feared the judgment seat he would soon be in front of. The last of Bearook's men were now fleeing in fear, their own hearts overwhelmed with doubts, their minds focused on what horrors there may be after death. Bearook was stunned by the expressions of the Kings men and began to scream in a mad rage. "Don't pity me you fools, I have conquered this world by my own hand, before this night is over my Gods will give me your flesh." One by one the Kings men began to put out the torches they had lit as they stared towards Bearook. The savage full of hate and fear once more had his sight taken away as he held his axe up towards his face. Bearook then found himself in the middle of the camp swinging madly for he could not see anything in front of him. He then screamed "show yourself, are you a coward, are you afraid of the great Bearook, Fight me!" Drac allowed the great green mist to glow from his body so his enemy could see him. Drac had been floating above Bearook and now landed some 10 feet in front of the savage. Bearook began to charge him swinging his axe towards his chest.

The axe struck the prince and his chest was opened which made Bearook laugh with pride at his accomplishment. His laughter turned quickly to fear as he watched the green mist coming from Drac's chest closing the wound and healing him completely. Bearook enraged charged once more with the ax and swung it towards Drac's chest but this time it was stopped by bat like claws. Bearook stared at Drac as the prince began to smile with his hideous monster like features then with a slight squeeze, the ax shattered into hundreds of pieces. Bearook yelled "What sorcery is this!" Prince Drac then spoke in his monstrous voice "Humble yourself Bearook, surrender and I will spare your life. You'll live the rest of your days in a prison, a living reminder to all those who choose wickedness over compassion," Bearook then thought to himself "Mercy; this fool wishes to give me mercy. Yes, this may be away for me to fight another day." He then said as he fell to his knees. "Yes, my Lord, my wicked ways are more than I can bare, give me mercy today and I'll live to be a better man. If I had a great King like yourself, I know that I could be worthy of changing my life." Even at that moment in Bearook's heart he was thinking of a way to kill the Prince. Drac then said "Rise Bearook, your words can easily hide the intentions of your heart, men can be so easily fooled by the flattery of praise that feeds their flesh. But there is one who can see the hearts of men and is not so easily fooled by their selfish intentions."

Drac now with an expression of great fear and sadness then said, "So why Bearook have you still chosen to harden your heart as death comes for you" Bearook then said frighten and confused "My Lord, what do you mean?" Drac stood in silence as the trees surrounding them began to stir, you could feel the wind's power growing with every second. The trees began to bend and crackle from the force moving through them. The Prince allowed the green mist to give light to the battlefield; the King and his soldiers were amazed at what was taking place around them. Then Drac said this to the savage Bearook as he lowered his head in despair "Your motives that were hidden in darkness have now been brought to light." Bearook screamed frantically as he could feel the vibrations from the trees moving closer to where they were. "What do you mean my lord, my lord, what do you mean?" Drac would not look up towards him. Then the savage ran towards the Prince and grabbed him begging "My lord, what is it?" At that time the most unforgettable expression of fear began to grow on the face of Bearook as the great wind seem to grow even stronger shaking the ground around him as if the land was about to open and swallow the savage whole. The mad barbarian then began to scream "Well then come for me, do you hear me, come for me!" Before Bearook could scream another word, the great Bat Kings claws had surrounded him, the Great bat saw that his heart had hardened to the point where he would never change. Bearook became pale almost lifeless as those massive talons began to tighten their grip. The great Bat King was removing this wicked man so that the land could begin to heal from all his wicked deeds. The Kings men became fearful for their own lives as they watched Bearook being taken by the massive beast. They knew at any time that if this creature was to turn on them there would be nothing they could do to save themselves. But a peace began to grow in their hearts, one that couldn't be explained, and they knew for whatever reason that the great creature would not come for them.

The Prince raised his head and watched Bearook being carried away through the clouds into the night sky and said quietly to himself "Thank you great Bat for freeing us from this wicked man and for this incredible gift you have given me. I will continue to protect the weak and serve others humbly with my Lord's help." Then the Great Bat King communicated back to Drac "Prince I know you will, please also continue to take care of my little one." Drac smiled and bowed his head in great respect then said, "I dare for someone to try and stop me." At that moment little Zip flew in and landed on Drac's shoulder and the Prince said to his small friend "Why do I have the feeling little one that I have you to thank for all of this." Zip smiled as his razor-sharp teeth could be seen and he then flew up underneath the Princes monster like chin as Drac carefully scratched the back of his head. The clouds began to move revealing the light of a full moon as everyone looked to the sky. But then they all became astonished as the moon began to shine on figures flying in their direction. They now could see thousands upon thousands of monstrous bats larger than any man coming towards them on the battlefield. The Kings men raised their weapons in fear and were prepared to fight if these creatures were coming to do them harm. As the King watched these creatures flying towards them it was as if he were a young man again on the day of battle when the dragons filled the sky. Drac's father with his great wisdom said "Men have you not seen the signs as I have, we live today because of the father of these massive creatures. Lower your weapons and give honor to his children." All the Kings men lowered themselves on one knee, bowing their heads in honor of the great beast. As the monstrous bats began flying in you could see them removing the bodies of Bearook's men from the land. One of the youngest of the Kings army who had shown great valor had found himself on the battlefield far from the others. With his head still lowered he could feel and hear what sounded like a tree falling at his feet. The young warrior began to slowly stand up and raise his head. As he looked up he saw one of the great Bat Kings war commanders standing but inches away from where he now stood. He was amazed and terrified at what was before him; he could see the battle scars on the great beast. The Kings army were all in shock as they began to raise their heads wondering if the young man was about to be a late-night snack. The beast stood staring at the young man while breathing like a machine. The young warrior could feel the large Bat's hot breath blowing towards his face. Everyone watching wondered if the young man was still alive since he had not moved. The only sign that gave them any comfort was that they could still see him standing. As the war commander turned back and forth, he could see Bearook's men were being removed from the land by his winged brothers. The massive monster once more turned and fixed his eyes toward the young warrior. Without warning the Beast looked up towards the sky and gave a screech that brought the hairs on the young man's arms to full attention. The war commander then lowered his head towards the young warrior as the boy continued to stand perfectly still. The two stared for what felt like an eternity to the young warrior but then the large bat blinked both eyes and bowed his head slightly downward with respect.

Then with incredible force he began to fly away from the battlefield, the sinews connecting his muscular tissue created a windstorm that had the young warrior fighting to stay on his feet. Once the war commander had made some distance the massive windstorm began to die down and the young warrior looked up to his brothers in shock to what had taken place. Everyone was very still as they looked towards the young warrior but then in great excitement the Kings army raised their hands and began to cheer for what they had just witnessed. The young man still in disbelief to what had happen fell to the ground in a seated position and said, "I thank thee oh Lord that the beast did not find me pleasing to his appetite." Then with both hands finding their way to his head he then said, "I think when I get home, I'll become a farmer like my father." A large smile began to grow on his face as he thought of what he had survived. The cheers from his brothers in arms could be heard throughout the surrounding landscape. Zip was amazed of what his master had become and was very thankful that the great Bat King found him worthy of such a gift. Zip was quickly startled as he could hear the great Bat King speak into his heart "Remember my child this gift was given because of your meekness, never forget that." As Zip heard this, he felt unworthy to the Bat King's gracious words then snuggled up even closer under the prince's chin. Everyone had finally come out of the caves and stood watching the King and his Men walking down the hillside away from the battlefield. They could see a creature walking alongside the king and were startled by the beast; at that time no one knew it was the prince. Drac was able to control the new power he had been given but the transformation from monstrous bat creature to human would not come quickly. As he walked down the hillside the villagers could see his wings begin to move inwards finding their way back into the frame of the Prince. They were amazed to see his monstrous fangs and claws slowly retract back into his body. Then the green mist began to surround him once more it became so thick that no one could see him until he was completely transformed back into the Drac they all knew. When he walked out of the mist the villagers just stood there in shock for some time but then one spoke "The prince is a monster, who now will save us from the prince." Drac's father then spoke up quickly "friends you have nothing to fear from my son, he had to become this creature for there was no other way that we would have gained this victory." The villagers looked towards each other puzzled not knowing what to make of everything that had taken place. But then one of the village elders spoke up "The creature in our stories has given the prince this power, this power was used for our good to defeat these wicked savages, Drac is not evil." Then another spoke up "Yes Drac and these men have freed us, we should celebrate this victory." Then Drac's father announced, "Well then tonight we celebrate for in 3 days those that wish will be traveling to their new homes in Hungary." Everyone began to cheer and some with great excitement for their hearts were longing for a fresh start and a bright future. However, there were others who were still very thankful for the Kings wonderful offer but could not see leaving the only place they had ever known. Those that chose to stay planned on continuing the work of their fathers and bringing crops in during their season.

The King promised to those that stayed he would create a great clearing from his land to theirs and would still consider them apart of Hungary with full protection. Drac had made his way to his new bride and never once took for granted what he had been given.

The journey would be long and frightening for a few that had never left the village but after many weeks they reached the land of Hungary. The warriors and villagers that had witnessed the great supernatural event on the battlefield passed on stories to their family and children. As the stories continued to be passed on from person to person some of the truth was starting to fall through the fingers of those holding on to these tall tales. Several years later as the King was at his tower around dusk on All Hallows Eve remembering those saints that had fought beside him and were no longer present. He thanked the Good Lord that men and women like these were found in Hungary to ease the suffering of others in the Lords name. He then walked over to his window looking down towards his son, Kaitlyna, Zip and their children enjoying themselves at one of Hungary's festivals. The King laughed as he saw the children playing music for their father. At special times for the children Drac would dress up as a nobleman with a fine cape and dance to their music. He had lost any need of self-preservation when it came to how he looked to others. The prince had no idea when his gifts would be called upon again, so he cherished moments like these more than any other. The King back at the tower began to laugh as he watched the spectacle Drac was making of himself for the enjoyment of his family. Drac's father would often think about the son he almost lost due to his heart of self and was thankful to the Lord for this gift that was given.

Then suddenly one of the Kings scouts rushed into his presence and said, "My Lord I must speak with you urgently." He replied, "Rise my friend what is it." "My Lord stories are being told outside of our kingdom by both wicked and good-hearted men of a blood thirsty creature that sucks the life out of innocent men and women. They are saying that this evil is coming from these very halls; the evil they speak of is no other than your son Drac. The King began to laugh hysterically "My Lord" the scout replied. The King answered "My good and faithful servant we will not spread lie's concerning the great power that lives within this very castle. For this gift has protected Hungary from evils and wicked creatures that only come to others in their nightmares. But if stories are being told from simple minded men of a much worse monster, a monster with no conscience, no heart, a wicked creature only wishing to feed on anyone or anything that enters into its path, well then others wishing to take this land would think twice before going against such a creature, don't you think." Smiling the scout said, "Yes my lord, I guess that would make savages think twice if such a monster did exist." The scout bowed to the King, respectfully the King bowed in return as the scout left the tower. The King walked back to the window and looked towards his wonderful family as Zip flew in and landed on his shoulder, the King said, "Hello Zip" He then began to rub the top of Zip's head as a wide smile began to spread across the King's face, looking out the window he watched his son kiss his beautiful wife Kaitlyna.

The King then started to chuckle hysterically and said to Zip as the kiss continued "O my little one, doesn't she know that's the monster of Transylvania, he'll drink her completely dry." Then the King started laughing uncontrollably with such great force that Zip had to hold on tightly to his beard. Drac went on to be a great King and his people were in awe of the respect and honor that they were given by him. The Kingdom continued to prosper and those needing aid always found a friend in Hungary. Drac and Zip did find themselves in several other adventures defending the innocent against creatures and monsters far worse than Bearook, but those stories are for another time.

Printed in the United States
By Bookmasters